Meet **Captain Brainpower.**
He's a superhero toy.
When he activates his Magic Button,
he becomes **REALLY CLEVER.**

And this is **Mojo.**
He's a sweet toy mouse.

They are best friends, and tonight they are off on a **fun adventure** together.
Or so they think...

Captain Brainpower peeps out from the back of the truck.
"Blooming Brains!" he exclaims. "This road leads to the rubbish dump!"
"But that's the place where people go to throw away all their old junk," cries Mojo. "I hope we're not going **there!**"

But **UH-OH!** That's **exactly**
where they are going.
Nobody wants these poor toys
any more and now they are being
THROWN AWAY!
Look! Chucked onto a pile
of pongy old rubbish.

"I don't like it here," whispers Mojo. "I'm scared."
Captain Brainpower holds his friend's hand tightly.
"Don't worry," he says bravely. "I'll look after you."

But **UH-OH!** There's something in
the rubbish dump shed –
and it's **not** friendly.

Suddenly the shed doors burst open, and out crashes a colossal claw.

It snatches up poor Mojo.

HOLEY MOLEY! WHAT IS IT?

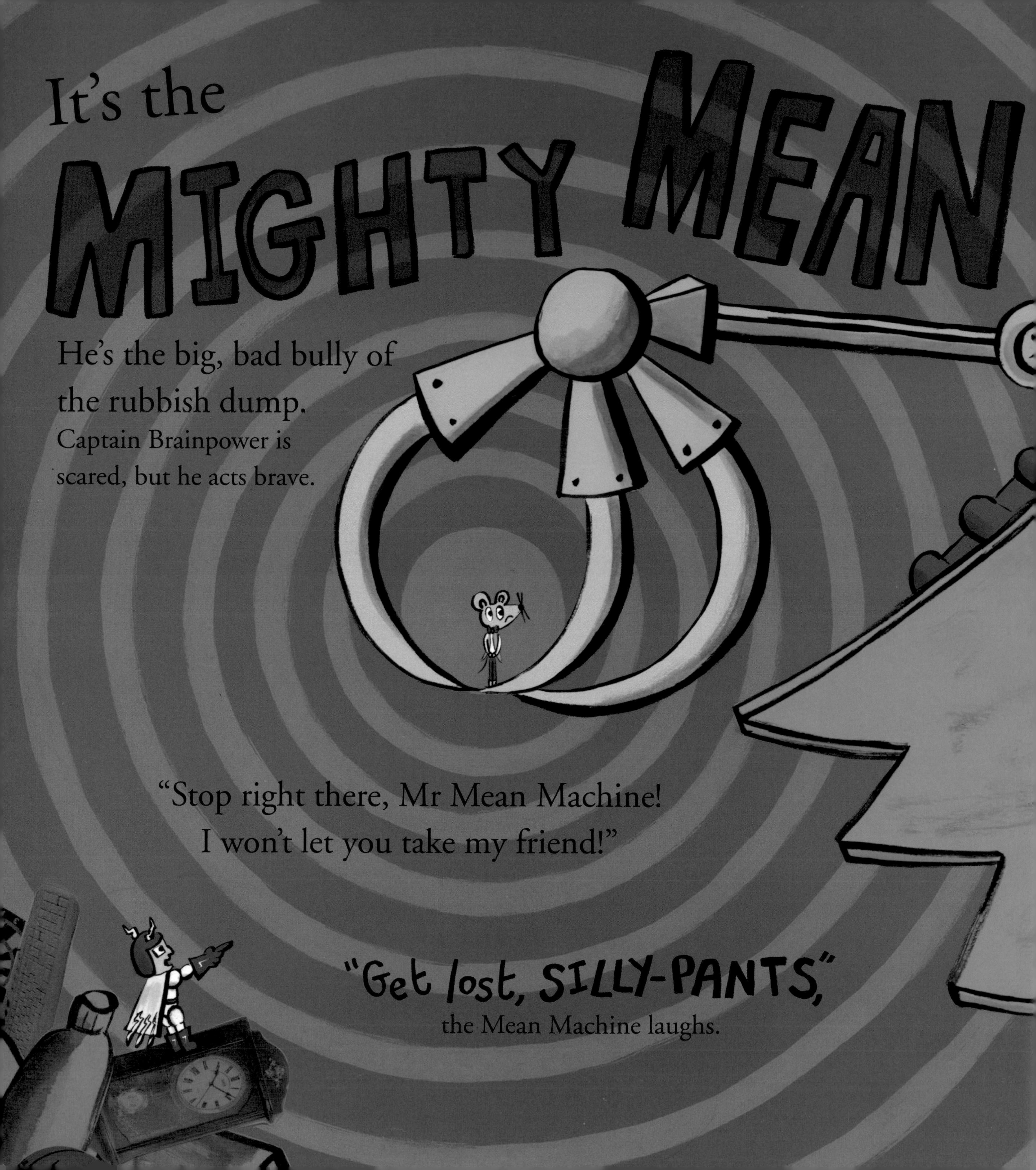

It's the MIGHTY MEAN

He's the big, bad bully of the rubbish dump. Captain Brainpower is scared, but he acts brave.

"Stop right there, Mr Mean Machine! I won't let you take my friend!"

"Get lost, SILLY-PANTS," the Mean Machine laughs.

MACHINE!
"Coz for breakfast,
what I love most,
is sausages, eggs
and MOUSE on toast!"

Captain Brainpower can only watch as the
Mean Machine carries poor Mojo back to the shed.
"Blooming Brains!" he gasps.
"It's not long until breakfast!
I have to rescue Mojo…
but **HOW?**"

If only he had...
SUPER STRENGTH,
A WEB SHOOTER
or
FLYING POWER!
Cor! If Captain Brainpower could fly, he could grab Mojo and zoom him to safety.
It's time to activate his **OWN** super power...

BRAIN POWER!
He pushes his Magic Button and shouts his special words, "GIVE ME BRAIN POWER!" And, Holey Moley! Look what's happening…
he's having a brainwave!
Click!
"IF I BUILD A PLANE, I CAN FLY!"

Captain Brainpower's brilliant brain scans the rubbish, **zooming in** on the special things he needs…
Fizzy burp
Marg
Low fat
CHEAPO
Crunchy Flakes

While the Mean Machine is snoring, Captain Brainpower sets to work, making a plane from bits of old rubbish.

He works hard and fast, all through the night.

At 7 o'clock in the morning (just before breakfast time), he finishes.

And here it is…

The BRILLIANT

But **UH-OH!**
Captain Brainpower can smell toast. The Mean Machine is starting to cook his breakfast!

BRAIN PLANE

cockpit is equipped with pilot ejector seat

lightweight fuselage = supreme speed

nose cone = flight stability

Captain Brainpower grabs his parachute.
"Hold on, Mojo! I'm coming!"

He fires up the engine!
ROARRRRR...
Speed
PARACHUTE
Pull toggle in EMERGENCY

Direction
Eject
3, 2, 1... BLAST OFF
Captain Brainpower to the rescue!

Up, up he zooms...high in the sky.
But the Mighty Mean Machine
hears him coming. He bashes
out of his shed, shouting,
"This mousey
is my breakfast!"

“Oh no he’s not!” shouts Captain Brainpower.

“Oh yes he is!” replies the Mean Machine.

“Well, look out then,” warns Captain Brainpower, **“because HERE I COME!”**

Captain Brainpower slams his foot on the accelerator!
The Brain Plane flies full speed…a million, billion, zillion miles an hour.
"Hey, Botty-Head! Catch me if you can!" calls Captain Brainpower, as he does some super stunts…

The Mean Machine gets MAD!
He tries to catch the Brain Plane,
but the more he chases,
the dizzier he gets.

Dizzier,

dizzier,
dizzier...

UNTIL...

BOOM!
BANG!
BLAHHHA!!
BASH!

He's
BAMBOOZLED!
What a blubbering hunk of junk!
"The Mighty Mean Machine indeed," giggles Captain Brainpower. "More like the Mighty Poopy-Pants!" And he scoops up Mojo from the Mean Machine's claw.
"Yippeeeee!!!"
cheer the toys.
"We're leaving this dump!"

But **UH-OH!**

The toys haven't noticed that they have a **BIG** problem…
"The Brain Plane's on fire!" cries Mojo. **"We're going to crash!"**
"BLOOMING BRAINS!" yells Captain Brainpower.
"Hold on tight!"

There's only one thing for it –
the gadget that no clever superhero
should ever be without
– **the emergency ejector
seat lever!**
YANK!
Direction
Ejector seat
The toys **shoot**
up into the air.
Captain Brainpower
tugs the
parachute
toggle…
C.B
and down
they drift…
down,
down,
down...
CHEAPO
back into…
CHE

…the stinky old **rubbish dump.**
"**Blooming Brains** and **botty burps,**" groans Captain Brainpower.
"**Now** what are we going to do?" sighs Mojo.
But **LOOK!** Captain Brainpower is activating his Magic Button.
He's having a…
MEGA MONSTER BRAIN WAVE!
PARACHU
CLICK

WE MUST MAKE
THE RUBBISH DUMP
OUR NEW HOME!!
"Are you bonkers?" gasps Mojo. "Why would we want to stay **here?!**"
"Well," explains Captain Brainpower, "there will be other toys who get thrown away, just like we were. They're going to need our help."
"By gosh, you're right!" agrees Mojo. "Brain Power is the **best super power EVER.**"

You see, if you use **YOUR** brain,
you can do **ANYTHING** – just like Captain Brainpower!
Look what he builds at the rubbish dump.

It's a...

SUPER SECRET DEN!

And this is where you'll find
the terrific twosome today.

As for the Mean Machine, he decides it's
more fun to be friends with Mojo than to eat him.
(He has jam on his toast for breakfast now.)
But there will **always** be other baddies out there, so…
if a toy is in trouble, don't worry…

it's Captain Brainpower and Mojo
to the rescue!